The Little Red Hen

Pictures by LUCINDA McQUEEN

SCHOLASTIC INC.
New York Toronto London Auckland Sydney

ISBN 0-590-41145-4

Text copyright © 1985 by Scholastic Inc.
Illustrations copyright © 1985 by Lucinda McQueen
All rights reserved. Published by Scholastic Inc.

Art direction by Diana Hrisinko
Book design by Emmeline Hsi

55 54   8

Printed in the U.S.A.

23

Once upon a time
there was a little red hen
who shared her tiny cottage with
a goose, a cat, and a dog.

The goose was a gossip.
She chatted with the neighbors
all day long.

The cat was very vain.

She brushed her fur,

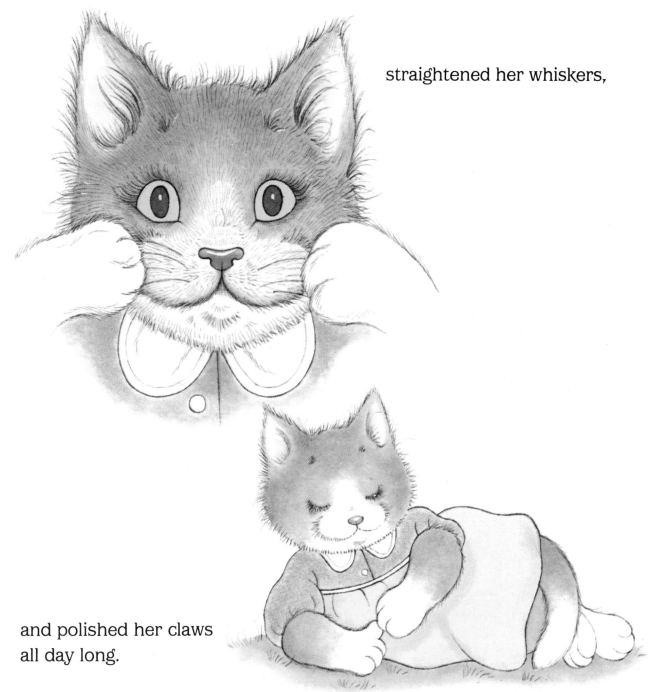

straightened her whiskers,

and polished her claws
all day long.

The dog was always sleepy.

He napped on the front porch swing
all day long.

The Little Red Hen
ended up doing
all of the work
around the house.

She cooked.
She cleaned.

She washed the clothes

and took out the trash.

She mowed the lawn
and raked the leaves.
She even did all of
the shopping.

One morning on her way to market,
the Little Red Hen found
a few grains of wheat.
She put them in the pocket
of her apron.

When she got home
she asked her friends,
"Who will plant these grains
of wheat?"

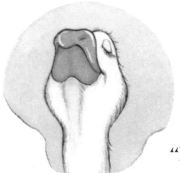

"Not I," said the goose.

"Not I," said the cat.

"Not I," said the dog.

"Then I will plant them myself,"
said the Little Red Hen.
And she did.

When the grains of wheat
began to sprout,
the Little Red Hen cried,
"Look, the wheat I planted is coming up!
Who will help me take care of it this summer?"

"Not I," said the goose.
"Not I," said the cat.
"Not I," said the dog.

15

"Then I will take care of it myself,"
said the Little Red Hen.
And she did.
All summer long she cared for the
growing wheat.
She made sure that it got enough water,
and she hoed the weeds out
carefully between each row.

By the end of summer
the wheat had grown tall.
And when it turned from green to gold,
she asked her friends,
"Who will help me cut
and thresh this wheat?"

"Not I," said the goose.
"Not I," said the cat.
"Not I," said the dog.

"Then I will cut and thresh it myself,"
said the Little Red Hen.
And she did.

When all of the wheat
had been cut and threshed,
the Little Red Hen scooped the wheat
into a wheelbarrow and said,
"This wheat must be ground into flour.
Who will help me take it to the mill?"

"Not I," said the goose.
"Not I," said the cat.
"Not I," said the dog.

"Then I will take it myself,"
said the Little Red Hen.
And she did.

The miller ground the wheat into flour
and put it into a bag for the Little Red Hen.

Then, all by herself,
she pushed the bag home
in the wheelbarrow.

One cool fall morning
not many days later,
the Little Red Hen got up early and said,
"Today would be a perfect day
to bake some bread.
Who will help me bake a loaf of bread
with the flour I brought home from the mill?"

"Not I," said the goose.   "Not I," said the cat.

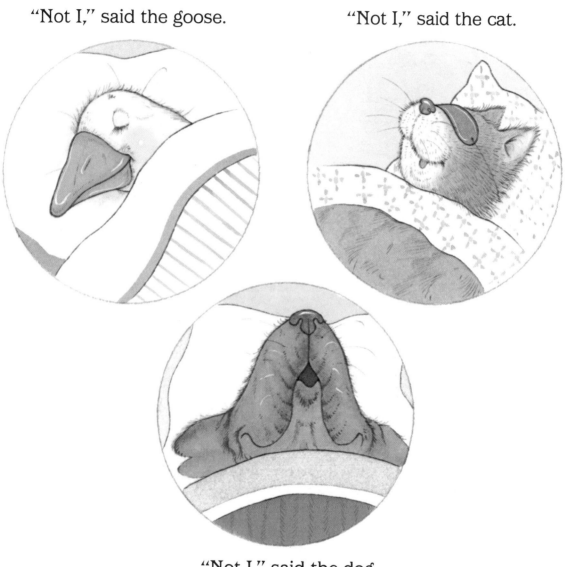

"Not I," said the dog.

"Then I will bake the bread myself,"
said the Little Red Hen.
And she did.

She mixed the flour with milk
and eggs and butter and salt.

She kneaded the dough

and shaped it into a nice plump loaf.

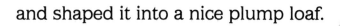

Then she put the loaf in the oven and watched it as it baked.

The smell of the baking bread
soon filled the air.
It smelled so delicious
that the goose stopped chatting...
the cat stopped brushing...

...and the dog stopped napping.

One by one they came into the kitchen.

When the Little Red Hen
took the freshly baked loaf of bread
out of the oven, she said,
"Who will help me eat this bread?"

"Oh, I will!" said the goose.
"And I will!" said the cat.
"And I will!" said the dog.

"You will?" said the Little Red Hen.
"Who planted the wheat and took care of it?
  I did.

Who cut the wheat?

Who threshed it and took it to the mill?
I did.

Who brought the flour home
and baked this loaf of bread?
I did.

I did it all by myself.
Now, I am going to eat it all by myself."

And that is exactly what she did.